Dear TABBY

by
Bruce Carlson

i

QUIXOTE
PRESS

Bruce Carlson
R.R. #4, Box 33B
Blvd. Station
Sioux City, Iowa
51109

iii

DEDICATION

to Cricket

TABLE OF CONTENTS

continued

TABLE OF CONTENTS - continued

FOREWORD

DEAR TABBY is a collection of whimsical letters from cats and dogs to advice columnist Tabby who has good advice for all who ask.

I think Bruce Carlson must be a cat or a dog, for no human could look at life quite like he has.

Prof. Phil Hey
Briar Cliff College
Sioux City, Iowa

PREFACE

Tabby, an advice columnist for cats and dogs, has shared with me, some letters from her files.

These letters, and her letters of response give us two-legged critters a new look at the lives of our pets.

Bruce Carlson

Dear Tabby,

I have a real problem. I was
sitting on a fence with a
calico friend of mine,
gnawing on some old fish
bones and just kind of hanging out.

As we were visiting, I saw a flea on
her back. She didn't know it was on
her, but it was. I know there was no

mistaking it for anything else. It was
a real live flea. I didn't say anything
about it at the time for fear of offending
my friend.

But, I've been bothered about it ever since. Should
I tell her or just ignore the whole thing? I know
she would die of embarrassment if she knew I
knew that she had fleas. I'm afraid our friendship
might well be jeopardized if I told her the truth.

Apprehensive in Springfield

Dear Apprehensive,

A real friend would tell and let the chips fall where they may. As you say, she is a friend. If she is a real one, she'll want to know.

I think she'll appreciate your having enough concern for her to do that.

Apprehensive, you need to have more faith in your friend and your friendship.

Tabby

Dear Tabby,

I'm a Collie dog, and I guess I'm a little more naive than I should be.

A Scottie moved in down the street, and we've gotten to be pretty good chums.

Not thinking very much, I showed the Scottie where I had buried several of my old bones and told him he could dig them up now and then and gnaw on them if he wanted.

But, now I've got a problem. Scottie has been digging those nice bones up and leaving them lay, even hauling them off, and not bringing them back.

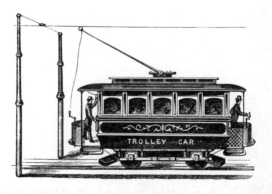

A couple of those bones were really kind of special, coming out of real nice juicy hams. One of those ham bones got drug out into the street where a trolley car dripped oil all over it.

Two more bones are just plain missing, and I feel terrible about it. What can I do?

A Sad Collie

15

Dear Sad Collie,

Of course, you know you can move the bones to some place your new "friend" doesn't know about, and then not be so free with telling folks where they are.

I am not advising you to do that, however. Your telling the Scottie about the bones and your invitation to dig them up and gnaw on them more or less makes them a gift to the Scottie. It would be kind of tacky to take those gifts back by hiding them again. I think you need to face the fact that your generous instincts have cost you your treasures. Better luck next time.

Tabby

Dear Tabby,

I have a problem with knowing how to handle my boyfriend.

I haven't had boyfriends before and am an orphan.   My mother was taken

to an animal shelter, and I have no idea who or where my father is. So, I don't get any guidance at home.

16

My problem with Scooter is that we have a date tonight. We're going to be going to a dogfight, and then do some scrounging around in a dumpster before coming home.

So, you see, it's going to be an ordinary sort of date.

My problem is that I know Scooter is going to want to rub noses when he sees me home, and I don't know if I should or not on the first date. What do you think?

Scared

Dear Scared,

A friendly little nose rubbing wouldn't be out of line under those circumstances.

If it goes beyond that, however, I'd suggest a cheerful good night and ducking into the house with a friendly wave.

If he is worth a second date, he'll understand and respect your wishes.

Tabby

Dear Tabby,

My husband has been working with our two young pups, teaching them how to chase cars.

When I suggest he give our little female pups a few pointers, he replies that little girl pups don't

need to learn how to chase cars.

I think that attitude is unfair.

A Concerned Reader

Dear Concerned Reader,

Such an attitude in these days is cruel, chauvinistic, and old-fashioned. If he continues to refuse to help the girls, you might want to suggest counseling. If he won't go, you might go without him. It will help you to cope with the situation.

You might also contact your local family support goup for help. I do hope you have success in your efforts.

Tabby

Dear Tabby,.

I seem to drool excessively,
especially around feeding time.
Do you have any suggestions?

Bernard

19

Dear Bernard,

It seems to me that a good check by a competent vet would be in order. If there is a physical reason for your drooling, perhaps he or she might be able to offer some relief with medication or other treatment.

If no physical reason is found, it might be appropriate for you to seek some professional counseling. I'm sure you can find a drooling support group in your area.

Tabby

Dear Tabby,

My new girlfriend, Wiggles, invited me over to her place to roll around in what was left of a dead animal of some sort that she had drug in from the woods.

So, I did. We both rolled around in it and really enjoyed ourselves. We stunk really, really good by the time we got done.

Then, later, I found out from the neighbor that

she hadn't drug that animal in at all. It had been drug in by a previous boyfriend, some hound dog she had picked up with.

I really felt awkward, having rolled around in an animal an earlier boyfriend had drug in.

Do you think Wiggles owes me an apology?

Mortified in Minneapolis

Dear Mortified,

I think you need to try to figure out if Wiggles' intention was a simple invitation from a sincere girlfriend, or if it was an attempt to embarrass you.

If you feel Wiggles wanted to embarrass you, it

might be prudent to look around the neighborhood for other young ladies.

Tabby

Dear Tabby,

I have a question about manners. Is it polite to lick your feet in public after a nice meal?

FiFi

Dear Fifi,

Licking your feet is quite appropriate under all social circumstances.

Tabby

Dear Tabby,

Ever since our new neighbor moved in, Tom seems to smile a lot in his sleep. I think she is the reason since he never did that before.

In fact, just last night, when he was fast asleep, I whispered her name in his ear. Sure enough! He started to smile.

Can I hold him responsible for what he does when he's asleep? Should I confront him with the evidence?

A Concerned Calico

Dear Concerned Calico,

What evidence? Why did he start to smile? Was it because of her name or was it your own sweet voice he responded to?

Try whispering "squash" to him the next time

23

you can catch him fast asleep. If he smiles, then it must be your voice that turns him on. If he doesn't smile, your suspicions might be justified.

Lots of luck. I do hope when you say *"squash"*, he grins ear to ear.

Tabby

Dear Tabby,

It's my wife. Just the other evening when I was sound asleep, that crazy feline leaned over in bed and whispered
"Squash"
in my ear. I let her know in no uncertain terms that it sure looks like she is slipping a cog and that she had no business waking a fellow out

of a good sleep to whisper *"squash"* in his ear. After all, I deserve my sleep just as much as anybody else.

Do you think I ought to have her talk to our preacher or someone who can straighten her out? I don't need any more of that foolishness.

A Tired Husband

Dear Tired Husband,

Don't bother me with your stupid questions .... you low-down, no-good alley cat!!

Tabby

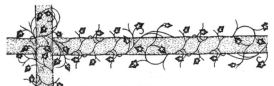

Dear Tabby,

Both my parents spend every week-
end spaced out over catnip. I'd like to
have some friends over now and then,
but don't dare for fear of my parents
embarrassing me to death. There isn't
anywhere we can hang out so I'm left
without any social life at all.

What can I do?

Lonely in Milford

Dear Lonely in Milford,

You are certainly to be commended for having to put up with such circumstances. Would it work to have friends over during the week?

Or, maybe you could meet over a garbage can, or somewhere else. I do wish you the best of luck for having to find friends under such trying conditions. Write and let me know how things work out for you.

Tabby

Dear Tabby,

My girlfriend, Fluffy, and I spent the weekend in a motel.

Then, yesterday, just two days later, my front leg

and right shoulder are kind of sore and swollen up.

Do you suppose I have cat scratch fever, and would it show up that soon, making my leg and shoulder hurt?

Troubled

Dear Troubled,

It sounds like you have a more serious problem than cat scratch fever, you undisciplined and corrupt alley cat. If you do have cat scratch fever, I hope it hurts like all get out.

Are you sure you aren't some kind of skunk or weasel?

Tabby

Dear Tabby,

I'm not trying to be an uppity sort of dog, but I do come from a long line of purebred poodles, and I know my master has plans on my having a nice litter of poodles for him.

Things happen, though, you know, and my friendship with a "Heinz 57" from down the block sort of got out of hand.

My master doesn't know it yet, but I am expecting, and the pups I'm going to have are going to be a far cry from purebred poodles. What shall I do? I've been thinking about running away from home, but I know I can't make it on my own out there in the wild.

A Sadder But Wiser Poodle

Dear Sadder,

There hasn't been a dog alive who hasn't made at least one serious mistake in his or her life. I think your master will be disappointed, but will realize that.

I would suggest you turn over a new leaf and learn to live a squeaky clean life after the arrival of the puppies. I think that when your master sees you are attempting to live up to his expectations, he will forgive you. You also need to forgive yourself, and to get on with your life. I do hope you have some nice pups and give them all the love they deserve.

Tabby

Dear Tabby,

I've just recently left the den and am trying to make it on my own. My desire is to learn the skills necessary to be a stand up comic.

A fellow who runs an exotic food restaurant offered me an opening this week-end there at his place of business.

Should I take this opportunity?

A Funny Feline

30

Dear Funny Feline,

An exotic foods restaurant, indeed!

My advice is to steer clear of that restaurant and not to turn your back on anyone hanging around with a cleaver in his hands.

Tabby

Dear Tabby,

Lots of young dogs
have medical problems of one kind
or the other these days.

Mine is that I have a hairball in
my stomach. I guess it might have
been from my being too diligent in
grooming myself as a little pup.

There is no reason for me to think
that the hairball will ever give me
any problems, but I do have it.

My problem is that I don't know if I
should tell my girlfriend about it. What

31

do you think?

Trying to be Honest

Dear Trying,

Your obvious resolve to be honest and forth-right is certainly commendable. Your girlfriend is fortunate in having a boyfriend like yourself. However, I don't know that your having a hair-ball is any reason for you to be making any kind of confession to her. If it would put your mind at ease to do so, go ahead and tell her. However, I can't think of any reason that a girl would have to be concerned about such a thing.

Tabby

Dear Tabby,

When I am dun with my nin lives, wil I have nin gosts? Why do us litle girl kitties have wiskers, and were do litle kitties cum from?

Wundering

Dear Wondering,

Thank you for the nice letter, Honey. What I think you need to do is to have a nice long talk with your mother about all those things. And you can suggest to her that if she has any trouble with your last question, there are good books at your local library about that.

And, be sure to write back to me if you don't get some answers to your questions.

Tabby

Dear Tabby,

I don't know who else to turn to, so I am writing to you.

I'm so embarrassed about my mother. She's a widow cat and has quite a few boyfriends that come to see her; sometimes three or four different ones every week.

33

Mother and her friends will perch out on the wood fence around the yard where we live. They'll holler and carry on something unbelievable all night.

What can I do?

Embarrassed

Dear Embarrassed,

Sitting on a wooden fence doesn't come naturally and can take a little practice.

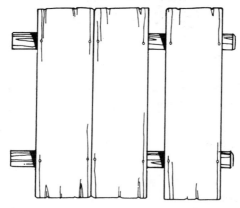

I'd suggest your working on getting a firm grip on the top of the board with your front feet and then sort of balancing yourself with your back feet.

There is no point in being embarrassed about it; you'll catch onto it in a short time if you practice.

Tabby

Dear Tabby,

My father is into violins. He has, in fact, really put himself in one of them. What do you think of that?

Proud in Pittsfield

Dear Proud in Pittsfield,

That's an old joke, and I'm not going to fall for it.

Tabby

Dear Tabby,

I'm the only dog in this neighborhood with rhinestones on my collar. Some of the others fellows have been teasing me about that.

How can I tell them that I can't help what my master decides to put on me for a collar?

Perplexed

35

Dear Perplexed,

You don't need to tell them anything.
That's why God gave dogs legs with
claws. Some vigorous scratching should
solve your problem.

Tabby

Dear Tabby,

I have a problem about territory.
I do a pretty good job of keeping my
territory marked. So does the neighboring dog.

We have both used a tree at the edge of our
territories. The problem is that the owner of the
land cut it down and there are no fire hydrants,
posts, bushes, or anything else we can use. All
that remains of that really convenient tree is a
lowly stump that is all but invisible there in the
long grass. We're at a real loss to know what to
do about the whole thing. Unless we keep our

36

territories well marked, there is always the possibility of disagreement and argument.

Without a Boundary in Springfield

Dear Without a Boundary,

Your well-written letter certainly makes it sound as if both you and your neighbor are

reasonable and sensible dogs. If that is true, you two should have no problem in resolving your problem.

While you may feel it is a bit demeaning, you might, of course, continue to use the remains of that tree stump.

Another solution might be for the two of you to find some relatively large object that you could drag to the site and use that. Perhaps a cardboard box or a limb would do.

I do wish you and your neighbor lots of luck in coming up with a suitable solution to your dilemma.

Tabby

Dear Tabby,

I have a real problem. Our fourth to the last girl of our fifth litter has fallen in with a young tom cat WHO BELONGS TO A VET!!

I suppose a cat can't be blamed for who he belongs to, but it is certainly disconcerting. As far as talking to the girl, I might as well talk to a wall. She doesn't seem to realize how mortified her relatives all are about her taking up with a vet's cat.

What do you suggest?

Mortified in Mapleton

Dear Mortified,

Fourth to the last girl of your fifth litter!!! It sounds to me that you should be thinking more in terms of some restraint on your part rather

than who's the owner of one of your kitten's boyfriends.

Perhaps, in fact, that vet might do your family some good in terms of population control.

I suggest that you find some other issue to get all bent out of shape about!

Tabby

39

Dear Tabby,

It's the two youngest Toms of my second litter. I'm at my wit's end, not knowing what to do about them. They are always pulling one practical joke after the other.

Just the other day, for example, they put some itching powder in the litter box.

Believe me, when you've picked up some itching powder from a litter box, you've got yourself a real problem.

I know this isn't a good representation of a cat,
but you try using a litter box with
itching powder in it and
see how you look!

Needless to say, the whole situation has been a real source of stress to all of us around here.

We have no idea of where they got the itching powder, and the boys won't say. I think there might well be a dealer working at or near their obedience school.

What do you suggest?

Distressed

Dear Distressed,

First of all, I'd either get those boys to reveal the source of their itching powder or make them wish they really had.

If they were my kittens, they'd have just so many minutes to come up with the information, or I'd lower the boom on 'em.

Second, I'd avoid that litter box like the plague until your owner changes the litter in it.

Believe me, I know full well that raising little toms can be a real chore. Lots of luck.

Tabby

Dear Tabby,

My problem is my parents. For some reason they've taken it upon themselves to get all uptight about my haircut.

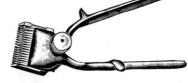

I'm proud of my hair style and I spent a lot of my own money on it. I don't see why they should care about how I wear my hair.

What I've done is a mohawk over my head, and a series of corn rows down along my back and sides. Then I topped it all off with an old-fashioned DA on my backside.

To me, it all looks cool, and I don't like the hassle I get from both Mom and Dad.

Happy with His Hair

Dear Happy,

There must be some mistake .... cats don't get haircuts. Or do they now? Maybe I have something to learn.

Would you send me a photo of yourself with your fine haircut? I'll respond to your letter again after I've seen the photograph.

Tabby

Dear Tabby,

I am a black and white cat and live here in Illinois on a busy highway.

Because that highway is so busy, a lot of rabbits and other animals get run over on that road, and end up as roadkill.

43

Needless to say, I and my litter mates take full advantage of the nice delicious goodies out there on the road.

Some of them get kind of squished and flattened, but they are still tasty.

Lately, though, we've run into a problem that we hadn't had before. A big old Tom from across the river over in Iowa has been coming to the highway in front of our place and eating our roadkill. Not only that, but he's been piggy about it and chases us off.

Is that right? Shouldn't we have first dibs on that roadkill since it's in front of our place?

Angry in Illinois

Dear Angry,

You didn't mention if the highway was a state road or an interstate. If it's an interstate, that

44

cat from Iowa has just as much right on it as you do. If it's a state road, I think you need to put your foot down since you do live in Illinois.

Tabby

Dear Tabby,

Is it OK to pet on a first date?

A Concerned Kitty

Dear Concerned Kitty,

Such a question from a cat! Is there a cat alive who is not in favor of petting at anytime whatsoever?

Tabby

Dear Tabby,

I'm a cat with splotches of yellow, black and white. My mother has always been so proud of my many colors that she named me Calico.

But, now a snooty cat from the next block claims I don't deserve that name because you have to have four colors to be a calico cat.

Not only has that snooty cat been giving me all

45

that grief, but she has only two colors herself.

I think I'm a calico cat, so what can I tell that uppity cat from the next block?

A CALICO? CAT

Dear Calico Cat,

I'm happy to report you can carry your name with all the pride you feel, because you *are* a calico cat. Some folks believe you have to have four colors to be a calico, but you don't. As long as you have splotches of color, you're a calico. Look it up in the dictionary.

Happily Yours,

Tabby

Dear Tabby,

Last week, my boyfriend gave me a friendship collar. It's not an engagement collar, just a friendship one.

I was examining it closely the other evening when I took it off as I was getting ready to go to bed. The collar is set off with some really nice lace, and a little lace bow. It really does look nice.

But, what bothers me is that I noticed that it is all built around an existing collar, a flea collar!

I was dismayed to see that. Maybe that flea

collar was just a convenient thing to start with, but I don't know. Maybe he was trying to tell me that I have been bothered with lice or fleas, and it hurts me to think that he might think that of me.

What should I do? I'm of a mind to return the collar to him and tell him to get lost.

Hurt in Farmersburg

Dear Hurt,

Now, wait a minute. Let's look at this from his perspective. If it was just a matter of convenience for him to start his project with an existing collar, and it happened to be a flea collar, you can't blame him for that. If he was thinking that you could have good use for the flea repelling features of a flea collar, you have to admit he was most gracious about the way he got the job done. I'd vote him a hero, myself.

I'd suggest you look at the big picture and recognize you have a boyfriend a lot of cats would give one or two of their nine lives for.

Tabby

Dear Tabby,

We are planning a small, semi-formal wedding for our kitten, Cleo, and her fiance who is a nice young tom from a very good family in town.

Our family is inclined to mark the occasion by going to a good robust dog fight. The groom-to-be thought that would be out of place as part of a semi-formal wedding. We agreed to leave it up to you to decide.

A Wondering Mother

49

Dear Wondering,

Since your half of the family came up with the dogfight idea and the groom apparently has not, I'd suggest coming up with a compromise. Some of you could do the dogfight, and those so inclined could just hang around the litter box, take a nap, or whatever. The happy couple might make it a point to show up at both places to avoid any bad feelings on the part of any of the guests.

Tabby

Dear Tabby,

We are concerned about our pup, Tippy.

We've always known, of course, that when he got old enough, we'd have to face the problem of cars.

Well, Tippy is old enough now, and the whole car issue is thrust upon us. It is even worse than we had anticipated. He simply shows no interest in chasing cars. We've tried to shame him into it, bribe him, and threaten to take away privileges. Nothing seems to work. What would you do?

Fearful Parents

Dear Fearful,

Yours is not an uncommon problem. But be patient. Keep the lines of communication open and set good examples. Time will bring all things. I think you'll find your pup will soon be chasing cars like all the other fellows.

Tabby

Dear Tabby,

The youngest member of our last litter is especially difficult to raise. Not only

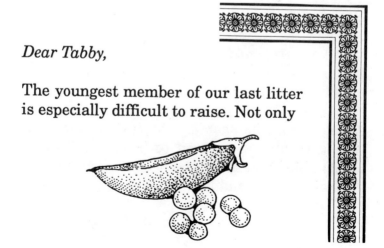

is he talking about being a vegetarian, but he is fixing his hair in really weird ways. He calls his haircuts by names I don't even understand, much less approve of.

We come from a long line of solid middle-classed mousers, and I'm just sick about that kid who seems to be revolting just for the sake of revolting. What can we do?

Tired of Weird Haircuts

Dear Tired,

Don't waste your energy and influence on things that don't really count. The hairdos will pass as he matures.

A vegetarian mouser is, however, in lots and lots of trouble. You need to have a calm and reasonable discussion about that. Concentrate on that problem and let the haircuts go.

Tabby

Dear Tabby,

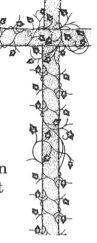

Tom and I have about decided we've had enough kittens.

I read an article recently in a magazine about how tomcats can get "fixed". We're thinking about going to a veterinarian to get Tom fixed.

At the same time, however, we don't want to burn our bridges behind us. Another article I read said the "fixing" can be reversed. Is that true? Can the fixing be reversed? Are there any dangerous side effects to the fixing?

Ready for a Rest

Dear Ready,

I think the basic problem is that you have been reading way too many magazine articles.

You let that veterinarian anywhere near your husband, and you'll think side effects!

Tabby

Dear Tabby,

I have a problem. Well, I think I have a problem. I'm not sure, but I think it is going on, and I have no way to prove it.

What I think is happening is my boyfriend calls me on the telephone without any clothes on. Don't ask me how I know that, I just seem to sense it.

Should I confront him with my feelings?
Should I talk to his parents? I just don't know
what to do but need to do something.
It is bothering me more all the time.

Apprehensive in Coaltown

Dear Apprehensive,

Try to think about this objectively.

It might interest you to know that the office I
am working in has myself, my secretary, two
assistants, a fellow working on the copying
machine, and four visitors.

Over half of us don't have clothes on at all. Just
remember, cats don't always wear clothes. It is

quite all right for your boyfriend to call you on the phone without any clothes on.

Maybe you would be more comfortable if you took your clothes off when he calls, so it would seem more natural.

Good luck.

Tabby

Dear Tabby,

It's about our little pussy cat. She is a real fast learner. For example, she learned to chase her tail earlier than our other kittens.

She is really too young to go to school yet if you just figure on her age. But, I am sure she could handle it.

Going to school early like this would give her a good head start in life, don't you think? Do you think I should insist with the school people that she be allowed to go early?

I've decided I'd abide by your suggestion about this.

A Concerned Mom

Dear Concerned Mom,

Your kitten's sense of well being, her kittyhood, and her happiness are far more important than a few weeks head start in school. I'd concern myself with what's right for her.

Think about it; maybe you're trying to impress your friends.

Tabby

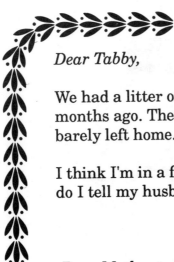

Dear Tabby,

We had a litter of kittens just a few months ago. The kids have, in fact, just barely left home.

I think I'm in a family way again. How do I tell my husband?

A Mother-to-be

Dear Mother to be,

I'd suggest you tell him the old-fashioned way.

Why don't you knit a couple dozen kitty socks? That ought to get the message across.

Tabby

Dear Tabby,

My boyfriend has a hang up about fish. He won't take me out to scrounge through any tempting dumpsters, or looking for dead birds, or anything like that.

He's a fish freak, through and through. Fish is all we eat, and that's all he'll treat me to. What should I do?

Tired of Tuna

Dear Tired,

Here's my idea. I think you ought to buy your boyfriend some fishing equipment and encourage him to take up fishing as a pastime.

In fact, he might find it useful to have something to take up some of his extra time. With any luck he'll have a lot of extra time if you use

your head and see if there are any other pebbles on the beach. His selfish behavior will do nothing but get worse with time.

Tabby

Dear Tabby,

My daughter is just as cute a little kitten as one could ask for. She is good-looking, intelligent, and has a great personality.

There is no reason whatsoever that she could not have whatever young tom she wanted chasing her.

But, to my real disappointment, she has

taken up with a neighboring puppy. Those two spend a lot of time together, and neither of them seems to have any other friends.

Cuddles says that the pup is just a friend, and that's all. But, I'm worried. Friendship can turn so quickly into romance, and those two are getting to be just at that dangerous age. Sometimes, in fact, I catch them looking at each other with that very special look.

What can I do?

Worried

Dear Worried,

I can understand your concern. But, you know how the brashness of youth can get them in trouble so quickly.

I'd suggest you might get used to the idea of grandchildren who wag their tails.

Tabby

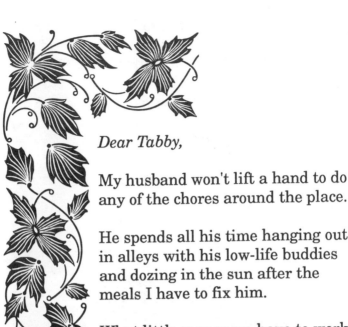

Dear Tabby,

My husband won't lift a hand to do any of the chores around the place.

He spends all his time hanging out in alleys with his low-life buddies and dozing in the sun after the meals I have to fix him.

What little money we have to work with is what I can take in by doing washing and ironing, something I've been doing so long that I've developed back trouble.

What would you suggest I do?

Tired and Weary

Dear Tired and Weary,

Without him.

Tabby

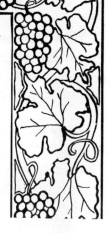

Dear Tabby,

We are really pretty poor alley cats. We can see no way for us to get ahead unless we win the lottery.

I saved up enough money to consult a fortune teller last week who told me that she could definitely see a big lottery win for me in my future.

This fortune teller told me that in order for that to happen, however, I had to do it exactly the way she instructed me.

She said I should sell everything I possibly could, borrow all I could, and do whatever else was necessary to raise as much money as I could possibly raise.

She said that all this had to be done in absolute secrecy; that it was very important that no one would know about it. She told me if anyone knew what I was doing, I would not win.

Finally, after buying the tickets, I am supposed to take them to her so she can cast good fortune on them for me. She said it would take her a day and a night to cast that good fortune on them.

What do you think?

Desperate

Dear Desperate,

I think that unless you wise up, you will be desperately poor the rest of your life.

For starters, there are two things you need to avoid at all costs. One is the lottery, and the other is conniving and crooked fortune tellers.

Tabby

Epilogue

Tabby, for all the cats and dogs who would write in with questions, always had some good advice.

Sometimes she'd be sympathetic and sometimes she'd say what had to be said .... whoever it might rub backwards.

Whatever advice Tabby gave, it was always sure to help someone over rough spots in life.

Need a Gift?

for

• Shower • Birthday • Mother's Day •
• Anniversary • Christmas•

Turn Page For Order Form
(Order Now While Supply Lasts!)

TO ORDER COPIES OF *DEAR TABBY*

Please send me .... copies of *Dear Tabby* at $5.95 each.
(Make checks payable to **QUIXOTE PRESS**.)

Name ....

Street ....

City/State/Zip..

Send Orders to:

QUIXOTE PRESS
R.R. #4, Box 33B
Blvd. Station • Sioux City, Iowa 51109

TO ORDER COPIES OF*DEAR TABBY*

Please send me ....copies of *Dear Tabby* at $5.95 each.
(Make checks payable to **Quixote Press**.)

Name ....

Street ....

City/State/Zip..

QUIXOTE PRESS
RR #4, Box 33B
Blvd. Station • Sioux City, Iowa 5110

Since you have enjoyed this book, perhaps you would be interested in some of these other paperback books from QUIXOTE PRESS

ARKANSAS BOOKS

ARKANSAS' ROADKILL COOKBOOK
  by Bruce Carlson...$7.95
REVENGE OF ROADKILL
  by Bruce Carlson...$7.95
GHOSTS OF THE OZARKS
  by Bruce CArlson..$9.95
ME'N IRWIN (how us Arkansas boys made our home-made toys from junk we'd find around)
  by Bruce Carlson...$9.95
A FIELD GUIDE TO SMALL ARKANSAS FEMALES
  by Bruce Carlson...$9.95
LET'S US GO DOWN TO THE RIVER 'N ...
  by various authors $9.95
ARKANSAS' VANISHING OUTHOUSE
  by Bruce Carlson...$9.95
TALL TALES OF THE MISSISSIPPI RIVER
  by Dan Titus..$9.95
LOST & BURIED TREASURE of the MISSISSIPPI
  RIVER - by Netha Bell & Gary Scholl..................$9.95
TALES OF HACKETT'S CREEK
  by Dan Titus..$9.95
UNSOLVED MYSTERIES of the MISSISSIPPI RIVER
  by Netha Bell...$9.95
101 WAYS TO USE A DEAD RIVER FLY
  by Bruce Carlson...$7.95
MY VERY FIRST
  by various authors $9.95
VACANT LOT, SCHOOL YARD & BACK ALLEY
  GAMES - by various authors $9.95
HOW TO TALK MIDWESTERN
  by Robert Thomas...$7.95

DAKOTA BOOKS

Some Pretty Tame, But Kinda Funny Stories About Early
DAKOTA LADIES-OF-THE-EVENING
by Bruce Carlson...$9.95
SOUTH DAKOTA ROADKILL COOKBOOK
by Bruce Carlson...$7.95
REVENGE OF ROADKILL
by Bruce Carlson...$7.95
101 WAYS TO USE A DEAD RIVER FLY
by Bruce Carlson...$7.95
TERROR IN THE BLACK HILLS
by Dick Kennedy...$9.95
GHOSTS OF THE BLACK HILLS
by Tom Welch $9.95
LET'S GO DOWN TO THE RIVER 'N,,,
by various authors $9.95
LOST & BURIED TREASURE of the MISSOURI RIVER
by Netha Bell..$9.95
MAKIN' DO IN SOUTH DAKOTA
by various authors $9.95
MEMOIRS OF A DAKOTA HUNTER
by Gary Scholl..$9.95
GUNSHOOTIN', WHISKEY DRINKIN', GIRL CHASIN'
STORIES OUT OF THE OLD DAKOTAS
by Netha Bell..$9.95
THE DAKOTA'S VANISHING OUTHOUSE
by Bruce Carlson...$9.95
MY VERY FIRST
by various authors $9.95
VACANT LOT, SCHOOL YARD & BACK ALLEY GAMES
by various authors $9.95
HOW TO TALK MIDWESTERN
by Robert Thomas...$7.95

ILLINOIS BOOKS
THE VANISHING OUTHOUSE OF ILLINOIS
by Bruce Carlson...$9.95
A FIELD GUIDE TO ILLINOIS' CRITTERS
by Bruce Carlson...$7.95

YOU KNOW YOU'RE IN ILLINOIS WHEN ...
by Bruce Carlson...$7.95
Some Pretty Tame, But Kinda Funny Stories About Early
ILLINOIS LADIES-OF-THE-EVENING
by Bruce Carlson...$9.95
ILLINOIS' ROADKILL COOKBOOK
by Bruce Carlson...$7.95
REVENGE OF THE ROADKILL
by Bruce Carlson...$7.95
101 WAYS TO USE A DEAD RIVER FLY
by Bruce Carlson...$7.95
TALL TALES OF THE MISSISSIPPI RIVER
by Dan Titus...$9.95
TALES OF HACKETT'S CREEK
by Dan Titus...$9.95
UNSOLVED MYSTERIES OF THE MISSISSIPPI
by Netha Bell..$9.95
LOST & BURIED TREASURE of the MISSISSIPPI
by Netha Bell & Gary Scholl $9.95
STRANGE FOLKS ALONG THE MISSISSIPPI
by Pat Wallace..$9.95
LET'S US GO DOWN THE THE RIVER 'N ......
by various authors $9.95
NUDE HUNTING IN ILLINOIS (some things to think
about while stompin' around Illinois' woodlands in the
bufff.) - by Bruce Carlson...$5.95
MISSISSIPPI RIVER PO' FOLK
by Pat Wallace..$9.95
GHOSTS of the MISSISSIPPI (from Dubuque to Keokuk)
by Bruce Carlson...$9.95
GHOSTS of the MISSISSIPPI (from Keokuk to St.Louis)
by Bruce Carlson...$9.95
MAKIN' DO IN ILLINOIS
by various authors $9.95
MY VERY FIRST
by various authors $9.95
VACANT LOT, SCHOOL YARD & BACK ALLEY GAMES
by various authors $9.95
HOW TO TALK MIDWESTERN
by Robert Thomas $7.95

IOWA BOOKS

IOWA'S ROADKILL COOKBOOK
by Bruce Carlson..$7.95
REVENGE OF THE ROADKILL
by Bruce Carlson..$7.95
IOWA' OLD SCHOOLHOUSES
by Carole Turner Johnston.................................$9.95
GHOSTS OF THE AMANA COLONIES
by Lori Erickson...$9.95
GHOSTS OF THE IOWA GREAT LAKES
by Bruce Carlson..$9.95
GHOSTS of the MISSISSIPPI (from Dubuque to Keokuk)
by Bruce Carlson..$9.95
GHOSTS of the MISSISSIPPI (Minneapolis to Dubuque)
by Bruce Carlson..$9.95
GHOSTS of the MISSISSIPPI (from Keokuk to St. Louis)
by Bruce Carlson..$9.95
GHOSTS OF POLK COUNTY, IOWA
by Tom Welch $9.95
TALES OF HACKETT'S CREEK
by Dan Titus..$9.95
ME'N WESLEY (stories about the homemade toys that
Iowa farm children made & played with around the turn
of the century) - by Bruce Carlson $9.95
TALL TALES OF THE MISSISSIPPI RIVER
by Dan Titus..$9.95
UNSOLVED MYSTERIES OF THE MISSISSIPPI
by Netha Bell...$9.95
101 WAYS TO USE A DEAD RIVER FLY
by Bruce Carlson..$7.95
LET'S GO DOWN TO THE RIVER 'N...
by various authors $9.95
TRICKS WE PLAYED IN IOWA
by various authors $9.95
IOWA, THE LAND BETWEEN THE VOWELS (farm boy
stories from the early 1900s)
by Bruce Carlson $9.95

LOST & BURIED TREASURE OF THE MISSISSIPPI
  by Netha Bell & Gary Scholl $9.95
Some Pretty Tame, But Kinda Funny Stories About Early
IOWA LADIES-OF-THE-EVENING
  by Bruce Carlson $9.95
THE VANISHING OUTHOUSE OF IOWA
  by Bruce Carlson $9.95
IOWA'S EARLY HOME REMEDIES
  by 26 students at Wapello Elem.School $9.95
IOWA - A JOURNEY IN A PROMISED LAND
  by Kathy Yoder $16.95
LOST & BURIED TREASURE of the MISSOURI RIVER
  by Netha Bell $9.95
FIELD GUIDE TO IOWA' CRITTERS
  by Bruce Carlson $7.95
OLD IOWA HOUSES, YOUNG LOVES
  by Bruce Carlson $9.95
SKUNK RIVER ANTHOLOGY
  by Gene Olson $9.95
MY VERY FIRST
  by various authors $9.95
VACANT LOT, SCHOOL YARD & BACK ALLEY GAMES
  by various authors $9.95
HOW TO TALK MIDWESTERN
  by Robert Thomas $7.95

KANSAS BOOKS
LET'S US GO DOWN TO THE RIVER 'N
  by various authors $9.95
LOST & BURIED TREASURE of the MISSOURI RIVER
  by Netha Bell $9.95
101 WAYS TO USE A DEAD RIVER FLY
  by Bruce Carlson $7.95
MY VERY FIRST
  by various authors $9.95
VACANT LOT, SCHOOL YARD & BACK ALLEY GAMES
  by various authors $9.95
HOW TO TALK MIDWESTERN
  by Robert Thomas $7.95

KENTUCKY BOOKS

GHOSTS of the OHIO RIVER (Pittsburgh to Cincinnati)
   by Bruce Carlson..$9.95
GHOSTS of the OHIO RIVER (Cincinnati to Louisville)
   by Bruce Carlson..$9.95
TALES OF HACKETT'S CREEK
   by Dan Titus..$9.95
LOST & BURIED TREASURE of the MISSISSIPPI
   by Netha Bell & Gary Scholl...................................$9.95
LET'S GO DOWN TO THE RIVER 'N...
   by various authors...$9.95
UNSOLVED MYSTERIES of the MISSISSIPPI RIVER
   by Netha Bell..$9.95
101 WAYS TO USE A DEAD RIVER FLY
   by Bruce Carlson..$7.95
TALL TALES of the MISSISSIPPI RIVER
   by Dan Titus..$9.95
MY VERY FIRST
   by Various authors...$9.95
VACANT LOT, SCHOOL YARD & BACK ALLEY GAMES
   by various authors...$9.95

MICHIGAN BOOKS

MICHIGAN'S ROADKILL COOKBOOK
   by Bruce Carlson..$7.95
REVENGE OF THE ROADKILL
   by Bruce Carlson..$7.95
A FIELD GUIDE TO SMALL MICHIGAN FEMALES
   by Bruce Carlson..$9.95
LET'S GO DOWN TO THE RIVER 'N
   by various authors...$9.95
101 WAYS TO USE A DEAD RIVER FLY
   by Bruce Carlson..$7.95
MICHIGAN'S VANISHING OUTHOUSE
   by Bruce Carlson..$9.95
ME 'N HERBIE (how us Michigan boys made our
homemade toys from junk we'd find around)
   by Bruce Carlson..$9.95
MY VERY FIRST
   by various authors...$9.95

VACANT LOT, SCHOOL YARD & BACK ALLEY GAMES
by various authors $9.95
HOW TO TALK MIDWESTERN
by Robert Thomas $7.95

MINNESOTA BOOKS

MINNESOTA'S ROADKILL COOKBOOK
by Bruce Carlson...$7.95
REVENGE OF THE ROADKILL
by Bruce Carlson...$7.95
A FIELD GUIDE TO SMALL MINNESOTA FEMALES
by Bruce Carlson...$9.95
GHOSTS of the MISSISSIPPI (from Minneapolis to
Dubuque) - by Bruce Carlson $9.95
LAKES COUNTRY COOKBOOK
by Bruce Carlson...$11.95
UNSOLVED MYSTERIES OF THE MISSSISSIPPI
by Netha Bell...$9.95
TALES OF HACKETT'S CREEK
by Dan Titus..$9.95
GHOSTS OF SOUTHWEST MINNESOTA
by Ruth Hein..$9.95
MINNESOTA'S VANISHING OUTHOUSE
by Bruce Carlson...$9.95
TALL TALES OF THE MISSISSIPPI RIVER
by Dan Titus..$9.95
ME 'N JAKE (how us Minnesota boys made our
homemade toys from junk we'd find around)
by Bruce Carlson...$9.95
Some Pretty Tame, But Kinda Funny Stories About Early
MINNESOTA LADIES-OF-THE-EVENING
by Bruce Carlson...$9.95
101 WAYS TO USE A DEAD RIVER FLY
by Bruce Carlson...$7.95
LOST & BURIED TREASURE of the MISSISSIPPI
by Netha Bell & Gary Scholl $9.95
MY VERY FIRST
by various authors $9.95
VACANT LOT, SCHOOL YARD & BACK ALLEY GAMES
by various authors $9.95

HOW TO TALK MIDWESTERN
  by Robert Thomas $7.95

MISSOURI BOOKS
MISSOURI'S ROADKILL COOKBOOK
  by Bruce Carlson...$7.95
REVENGE OF ROADKILL
  by Bruce Carlson...$7.95
LET'S US GO DOWN TO THE RIVER 'N...
  by various authors $9.95
LAKES COUNTRY COOKBOOK
  by Bruce Carlson...$11.95
101 WAYS TO USE A DEAD RIVER FLY
  by Bruce Carlson...$7.95
TALL TALES OF THE MISSISSIPPI RIVER
  by Dan Titus...$9.95
GHOSTS of the MISSISSIPPI (From Keokuk to St. Louis)
  by Bruce Carlson...$9.95
TALES OF HACKETT'S CREEK
  by Dan Titus...$9.95
STRANGE FOLKS ALONG THE MISSISSIPPI
  by Pat Wallace..$9.95
LOST & BURIED TREASURE of the MISSOURI RIVER
  by Netha Bell..$9.95
MY VERY FIRST
  by various authors $9.95
VACANT LOT, SCHOOL YARD & BACK ALLEY GAMES
  by various authors $9.95
HOW TO TALK MIDWESTERN
  by Robert Thomas $7.95
UNSOLVED MYSTERIES OF THE MISSISSIPPI
  by Netha Bell..$9.95
LOST & BURIED TREASURE of the MISSISSIPPI
  by Netha Bell & Gary Scholl $9.95
MISSISSIPPI RIVER PO' FOLK
  by Pat Wallace..$9.95
Some Pretty Tame, But Kinda Funny Stories About Early
MISSOURI LADIES-OF-THE-EVENING
  by Bruce Carlson...$9.95

GUNSHOOTIN', WHISKEY DRINKIN',GIRL CHASIN'
STORIES OUT OF THE OLD MISSOURI TERRITORY
   by Bruce Carlson..$9.95
THE VANISHING OUTHOUSE OF MISSOURI
   by Bruce Carlson..$9.95
A FIELD GUIDE TO MISSOURI'S CRITTERS
   by Bruce Carlson..$7.95
EARLY MISSOURI HOME REMEDIES
   by various authors $9.95
GHOSTS OF THE OZARKS
   by Bruce Carlson..$9.95
MISSISSIPPI RIVER COOKIN' BOOK
   by Bruce Carlson..$11.95
MISSOURI'S OLD HOUSES, AND NEW LOVES
   by Bruce Carlson..$9.95
UNDERGROUND MISSOURI
   by Bruce Carlson..$9.95

NEBRASKA BOOKS

DOWNHOME IN NEBRASKA (tales of a Nebraska
housewife) - by Madonna Walsh..............................$9.95
LOST & BURIED TREASURE of the MISSOURI RIVER
   by Netha Bell..$9.95
101 WAYS TO USE A DEAD RIVER FLY
   by Bruce Carlson..$7.95
LET'S GO DOWN TO THE RIVER 'N
   by various authors $9.95
SHE CRIED WITH HER BOOTS ON (tales of an early
Nebraska housewife)- by Madonna Walsh $9.95
MY VERY FIRST
   by various authors $9.95
HOW TO TALK MIDWESTERN
   by Robert Thomas..$7.95
VACANT LOT, SCHOOL YARD & BACK ALLEY GAMES
   by various authors $9.95

TENNESSEE BOOKS

TALES OF HACKETT'S CREEK
   by Dan Titus..$9.95

TALL TALES OF THE MISSISSIPPI RIVER
 by Dan Titus..$9.95
UNSOLVED MYSTERIES OF THE MISSISSIPPI
 by Netha Bell...$9.95
LOST & BURIED TREASURE of the MISSISSIPPI
 by Netha Bell & Gary Scholl $9.95
LET'S US GO DOWN TO THE RIVER 'N...
 by various authors $9.95
101 WAYS TO USE A DEAD RIVER FLY
 by Bruce Carlson...$7.95
MY VERY FIRST
 by various authors $9.95
VACANT LOT, SCHOOL YARD & BACK ALLEY GAMES
 by various authors $9.95

WISCONSIN BOOKS

WISCONSIN'S ROADKILL COOKBOOK
 by Bruce Carlson...$7.95
REVENGE OF ROADKILL
 by Bruce Carlson...$7.95
TALL TALES of the MISSISSIPPI RIVER
 by Dan Titus..$9.95
LAKES COUNTRY COOKBOOK
 by Bruce Carlson...$11.95
TALES OF HACKETT'S CREEK
 by Dan Titus..$9.95
LET'S US GO DOWN TO THE RIVER 'N...
 by various authors $9.95
101 WAYS TO USE A DEAD RIVER FLY
 by Bruce Carlson...$7.95
UNSOLVED MYSTERIES OF THE MISSISSIPPI
 by Netha Bell...$9.95
LOST & BURIED TREASURE of the MISSISSIPPI
 by Netha Bell & Gary Scholl $9.95
GHOSTS of the MISSISSIPPI (from Dubuque to Keokuk)
 by Bruce Carlson...$9.95
HOW TO TALK MIDWESTERN
 by Robert Thomas...$7.95
VACANT LOT, SCHOOL YARD & BACK ALLEY GAMES
 by various authors $9.95

MY VERY FIRST
by various authors $9.95
EARLY WISCONSIN HOME REMEDIES
by various authors $9.95
GHOSTS of the MISSISSIPPI (Minneapolis to Dubuque)
by Bruce Carlson..$9.95
THE VANISHING OUTHOUSE OF WISCONSIN
by Bruce Carlson..$9.95
GHOSTS OF DOOR COUNTY, WISCONSIN
by Geri Rider...$9.95
Some Pretty Tame, But Kinda Funny Stories About Early
WISCONSIN LADIES-OF- THE-EVENING
by Bruce Carlson..$9.95

MIDWESTERN BOOKS
THE MOTORIST'S FIELD GUIDE TO MIDWESTERN
FARM EQUIPMENT (Misguided information as only a
city slicker can give it) - by Bruce Carlson $5.95
VACANT LOT, SCHOOL YARD & BACK ALLEY GAMES
OF THE MIDWEST YEARS AGO
by various authors $9.95
HOW SOME OF US ITTY-BITTY FOLKS HERE IN THE
MIDWEST WOULD RUN A HOUSE IF WE HAD TO
by various authors $7.95
HOW TO TALK MIDWESTERN
by Robert Thomas...$7.95
MY VERY FIRST
by various authors $9.95
HITCH HIKING THE UPPER MIDWEST
by Bruce Carlson..$7.95
101 WAYS FOR MIDWESTERNERS TO 'DO IN' THEIR
NEIGHBOR'S PESKY DOG WITHOUT GETTING
CAUGHT - by Bruce Carlson $5.95

RIVER BOOKS
SKUNK RIVER AHTHOLOGY
by Gene "Will" Olson...$9.95
JACK KING vs. DETECTIVE MACKENZIE
by Netha Bell...$9.95

LOST & BURIED TREASURES ALONG THE
MISSISSIPPI - by Netha Bell & Gary Scholl...........$9.95
MISSISSIPPI RIVER PO' FOLK
  by Pat Wallace...$9.95
STRANGE FOLKS ALONG THE MISSISSIPPI
  by Pat Wallace...$9.95
GHOSTS of the OHIO RIVER (Cincinnati to Louisville)
  by Bruce Carlson...$9.95
GHOSTS of the OHIO RIVER (Pittsburgh - Cincinnati)
  by Bruce Carlson...$9.95
GHOSTS of the MISSISSIPPI (Minneapolis - Dubuque)
  by Bruce Carlson...$9.95
GHOSTS of the MISSISSIPPI (Dubuque to Keokuk)
  by Bruce Carlson...$9.95
GHOSTS of the MISSISSIPPI (Keokuk to St. Louis)
  by Bruce Carlson...$9.95
TALL TALES OF THE MISSISSIPPI RIVER
  by Dan Titus..$9.95
TALL TALES OF THE MISSOURI RIVER
  by Dan Titus..$9.95
RIVER SHARKS & SHENANIGANS (tales of riverboat
gambling of years ago) - by Netha Bell.....................$9.95
UNSOLVED MYSTERIES OF THE MISSISSIPPI
  by Netha Bell...$9.95
TALES OF HACKETT'S CREEK (1940s Mississippi
River kids) - by Dan Titus $9.95
101 WAYS TO USE A DEAD RIVER FLY
  by Bruce Carlson...$7.95
LET'S US GO DOWN TO THE RIVER 'N...
  by various authors $9.95
LOST & BURIED TREASURE OF THE MISSOURI
  by Netha Bell...$9.95

COOKBOOKS
ROARING 20's COOKBOOK
  by Bruce Carlson...$11.95
DEPRESSION COOKBOOK
  by Bruce Carlson...$11.95
LAKES COUNTRY COOKBOOK
  by Bruce Carlson...$11.95

A COOKBOOK FOR THEM WHAT AIN'T DONE A LOT
OF COOKIN'
  by Bruce Carlson...$11.95
FLAT-OUT DIRT-CHEAP COOKIN' COOKBOOK
  by Bruce Carlson...$11.95
APHRODISIAC COOKING
  by Bruce Carlson...$11.95
WILD CRITTER COOKBOOK
  by Bruce Carlson...$11.95
I GOT FUNNIER-THINGS-TO-DO-THAN-COOKIN'
COOKBOOK
  by Bruce Carlson...$11.95
MISSISSIPPI RIVER COOKIN' BOOK
  by Bruce Carlson...$11.95

MISCELLANEOUS BOOKS

DEAR TABBY (letters to & from a feline advice
columnist)
  by Bruce Carlson $5.95
HOW TO BEHAVE (etiquette advice for non-traditional
and awkward circumstances such as attending dogfights,
what to do when your blind date turns out to be your
spouse, etc.)
  by Bruce Carlson..$5.95
REVENGE OF THE ROADKILL
  by Bruce Carlson..$7.95